The Tooth

Avi Slodovnick

Manon Gauthier

Kane Miller
A DIVISION OF EDC PUBLISHING

Marissa's love of candy finally caught up with her. That morning, she woke up with a toothache, and instead of bringing her to school, her mother took her to the dentist.

Marissa didn't often go downtown. Columns of tall gray buildings cast great shadows across the streets. The sky, usually bright and blue, was barely visible between the rows of endlessly tall skyscrapers. Marissa and her mother walked hand in hand toward the dentist's office.

Men and women,
wearing long coats and long faces,
their collars up and their heads down,
rushed in every direction.
Marissa leaned close to her mother.

When they stopped at the corner,

waiting for the light to change,

Marissa noticed something unusual.

A man with a large nose and dark eyes

was sitting on a grate in the sidewalk.

In front of him was an open shoe box

with money inside.

Marissa had never seen anyone like him.

She wanted to take a closer look,

but her mother held her hand tightly.

As they crossed the street
to the dentist's building,
Marissa looked back
and watched the man
over her shoulder.
He sat quietly, watching
the people pass him by.

Up in the dentist's office,
they checked in with
the receptionist, who told them
to sit in the waiting room
until the dentist was
ready to see them.

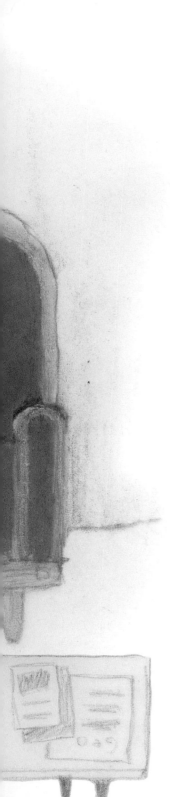

Marissa's mother sat down on the couch,

crossed her legs and

flipped through a magazine.

Instead of reading a book
or playing with a toy,
Marissa looked out the window
to the busy street below.
The man was still sitting on the grate.

Most people walked by the man.
Some people, just a few,
dropped coins into his shoe box.
One man in a hurry actually stepped
over the man.

Finally, after a long wait,

Marissa was called into

the examination room.

She sat in the big chair and

opened her mouth as wide as she could.

The dentist saw a small brown

hole in Marissa's tooth.

"That's quite a cavity," he said.

"The tooth will have to come out."

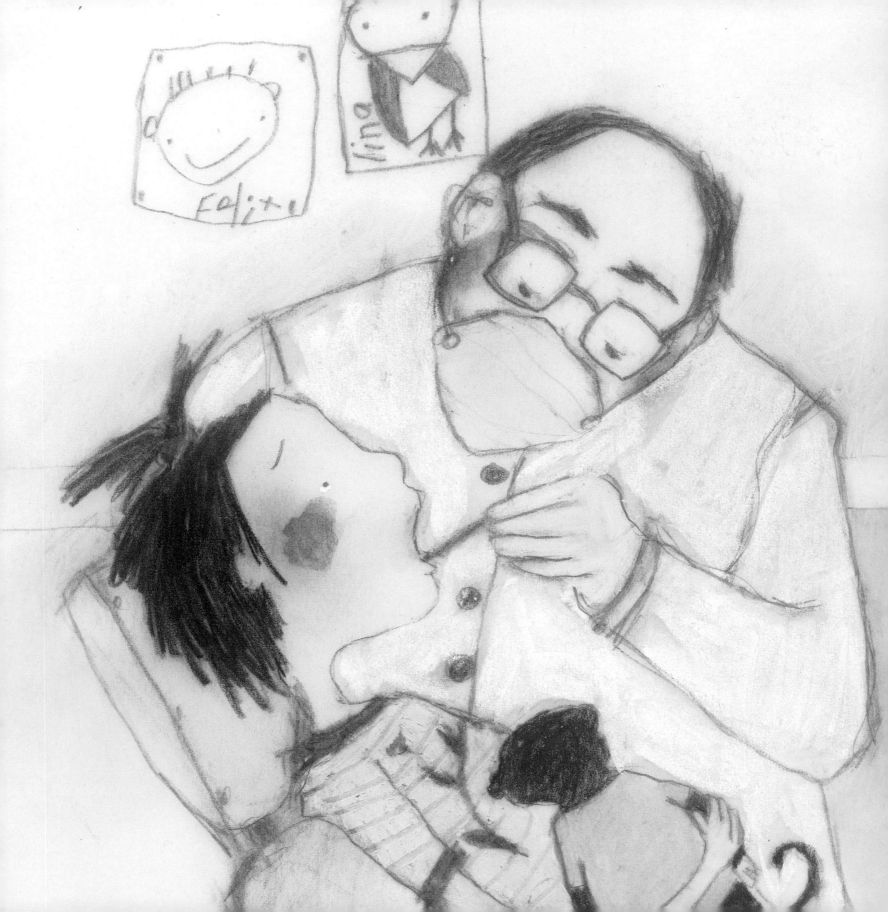

A few minutes later,
the dentist pulled out
Marissa's tooth.

Marissa wished she was in school.

"Here is your tooth, Marissa,"
said the dentist, slipping the tiny tooth
 into a small orange envelope.

"Make sure to put it under your pillow," said her mother.

"Make sure you brush your teeth twice a day,
and especially after candy!" said the dentist.

They left the dentist's office,
and in the elevator,
Marissa asked her mother,
"Is there really a tooth fairy?"

Outside the dentist's office,
the air was cool.
Marissa tickled the place
her tooth had been
with her tongue.
It felt funny.

They crossed the street.
The man was still sitting
on the sidewalk.

Marissa tried to get closer,
but her mother held
her hand tightly, like before.

Marissa pulled away and went up
to the shoe box.
There wasn't a lot of money inside.

Marissa held open the orange
envelope and let the tooth drop
into the shoe box.
"Put it under your pillow tonight," she told the man,
"and there will be money there tomorrow."

At first the man looked surprised.
Then he smiled warmly and waved
good-bye to Marissa as she
and her mother walked away.

Now all he needed…

...was a pillow.